Spirit Walker: Rise of The Astral Guardian

By: EJ Raman

D1715139

Copyright Page

Book title: Spirit Walker: Rise of The Astral
Guardian
Copyright © 2024 Elishiva Raman
All rights reserved.

Published by:
God's Way Publishing
Greensboro, NC

For permissions or inquiries, contact:
God's Way Publishing
https://sites.google.com/view/gwp2024/home
pegetahllc@gmail.com
+1 (336) 307-0188
Printed in the United States of America

Table of Contents

Dedication

To my family and loved ones,
Your unwavering support, prayers, and encouragement does not go unnoticed and is greatly appreciated.

To my readers,
This story is for you—those who believe in the triumph of light over darkness, who yearn for tales of courage, sacrifice, and faith. I pray that this journey inspires you to stand strong in the battles of life and to trust in the One who fights for us.

Above all, to my Heavenly Father,
I dedicate all my inspirational work to You, the Author and Perfecter of my faith. Thank You for blessing me with the gift of storytelling and for allowing me to use it for Your glory. May every word written reflect Your light, love, and truth. Without You, none of my stories would exist.

With love and gratitude,
Elishiva

Introduction: Hansin's Awakening

The cool breeze whispered through the dense foliage of the forest, carrying with it the sweet scent of pine and earth. Sunlight filtered through the canopy above, dappling the forest floor with patches of golden light.

Hansin Jasper, a young man of seventeen with tousled dark hair and piercing amber-brown eyes, sat beneath the towering trees, his mind adrift in a sea of tranquility.

Unbeknownst to Hansin, he came from a long line of Astral guardians, protectors of both the physical and Astral realms. His family's legacy was a secret carefully guarded by his great-grandmother, the last remaining keeper of their ancient heritage.

But for now, Hansin reveled in the simple pleasures of the natural world, unaware of the destiny that awaited him. As Hansin meditated, his thoughts were consumed by the sights and sounds of the forest around him. He found solace and peace in the quiet embrace of nature, unaware of the power that lay dormant within him.

Lost in the tranquility of the forest, Hansin's peaceful meditation was abruptly shattered by an unexpected surge of energy pulsating through his veins. Confusion and excitement intertwined in his mind as he felt the world around him shift and bend in ways he had never imagined. With a mix of trepidation and curiosity, he embraced the unknown, surrendering to the powerful force coursing through him.

In the blink of an eye, reality morphed into a realm beyond his wildest dreams. The air hummed with a mystical energy, and strange, fantastical beings floated past him in a mesmerizing display of ethereal beauty. Hansin stood in awe, his senses overwhelmed by the sheer wonder of this new world.

Suddenly, a spirit fox materialized before him, its eyes brimming with intelligence and a touch of surprise at the arrival of a new Astral guardian. Yuppi, as the fox introduced itself, became Hansin's guide in this enigmatic realm, shedding light on the urgent plight that had befallen their world.

Yuppi went on to tell Hansin about the dark ages the spirit realm had fallen into since the villain, Jezebell, had taken over. He explained how Jezebell, once a potential candidate to become an Astral guardian, was rejected due to her dark tendencies and thirst for power. Consumed by resentment and driven by a desire for revenge, she delved into forbidden arts, ultimately transforming into the malevolent entity known as the ethereal overlord.

For years, Jezebell wreaked havoc in both the physical and Astral realms, spreading fear and darkness with her corrupted touch. With her army of Phantom Legionnaires, she instilled terror wherever she went, corrupting souls and enslaving them to her will.

Recognizing the threat she posed, the previous Astral guardian managed to imprison Jezebell within a prison in the spirit realm. For decades, she remained trapped, her influence waning as the barrier between the spirit and physical realms held firm.

However, when the previous Astral guardian passed away without a successor, the barrier weakened, allowing Jezebell to break free from the prison but not outside of the realm with the aid of her minions. For seventy long years, she reigned unchecked in the spirit realm, spreading chaos and despair among its inhabitants.

Yuppi explained the urgency of Hansin's role as an Astral guardian and the dangers that lay ahead. Hansin listened in disbelief as Yuppi recounted the tale of Jezebell's fall from grace and her subsequent reign of darkness over the spirit realm. The spirit fox spoke of how Jezebell had twisted her powers to bend the very fabric of reality to her will, corrupting the once peaceful realm with her malevolent influence.

Here's a revised and enhanced version that retains the tone while deepening the descriptions and emotional intensity:

Here's the updated version with enhanced spiritual themes and a deeper focus on faith, trust, and hope in the Divine woven throughout:

Yuppi's voice trembled, a blend of sorrow and urgency weaving through his words as he recounted the devastation Jezebell had unleashed upon the spirit realm. Once a sanctuary of harmony and light, it had become a fractured and desolate shadow of its former self. Creatures that once roamed freely in unity now cowered in fear, their luminous essence siphoned away by Jezebell's insatiable hunger for power.

Hansin felt the weight of Yuppi's story settle heavily in his chest. A surge of determination flared within him, igniting like a spark in dry tinder, yet it clashed with an overwhelming sense of inadequacy. He was only seventeen—a boy with no knowledge of the supernatural, let alone the strength or wisdom to confront an ethereal force of darkness.

Still, beneath his doubts, a flicker of faith took root. It whispered to him, quiet yet unshakable, that his presence in the Astral realm was no accident. The Divine, in infinite wisdom, had summoned him here—not because of his strength but because of his willingness to act. Hansin's heart swelled with a fragile yet growing trust. The Divine's ways were higher than his own understanding, and he clung to the belief that the power to restore balance was not his alone. He was simply a vessel, guided by the greater hand of the Divine.

As the weight of his destiny pressed heavily upon his shoulders, Hansin lifted his chin. His amber-brown eyes glinted with newfound resolve, their light catching the faint luminescence of the forest around him. Though the path ahead was fraught with uncertainty, he didn't need to feel ready. He only needed to trust and take the first step, leaning on the strength of the Divine to carry him forward.

"I'll act in faith, I trust in the Spirit of the Divine." he murmured to himself, his voice steadying as the words settled into his soul. With determination rooted in trust and a heart burning with hope, Hansin vowed to face Jezebell and her darkness, not by his power alone but through the guidance and strength of the Divine.

Yuppi regarded him with solemn approval, sensing the internal shift within Hansin. The spirit fox's presence was a reminder that he was not alone, a tangible sign of the Divine's provision. Together, they would embark on this sacred mission to reclaim what was lost, not just for the creatures of the spirit realm but as a testament to the unwavering hope that even the darkest forces could not extinguish.

Hansin's steps carried him forward, his heart lifted by an unshakable truth: the Divine was with him. In that truth, he found the courage to face the trials ahead. For what power did darkness hold in the presence of faith, trust, and the light of the Divine?

"I'll do whatever it takes," he whispered, his voice firm despite the tremor in his heart. The words were a vow—not only to himself but to the realm that had placed its fragile hope upon him.

As Yuppi's tale drew to a somber close, an unspoken bond seemed to form between the young guardian and the spirit fox. The weight of their shared mission burned like a flame in Hansin's heart, tempered by the knowledge that he wouldn't face this battle alone. Yuppi, the steadfast guide, the untapped potential within Hansin and his faith were a threat against Jezebell's dominion and reign.

Chapter 1: Trapped in the Spirit

The golden hues of the setting sun filtered through the forest canopy, casting an ethereal glow upon the trees as Hansin's older brother, Keanu, stood at the edge of their home's clearing. *"Hansin! Dinner's ready!"* he called, his voice ringing through the tranquil woods. The aroma of their mother's cooking mingled with the crisp air, a warm reminder of home. But no response came. The stillness that followed was unsettling.

Keanu's brow furrowed as concern crept into his heart. Hansin often wandered the woods, but he was always back by nightfall. With each passing moment of silence, unease tightened its grip on Keanu. He stepped into the forest, his boots crunching against the leaves as he searched for his younger brother.

The deeper Keanu ventured, the darker the woods became, their shadows deepening with the fading light. His heart jolted when he finally spotted Hansin lying on the forest floor, motionless. *"Hansin!"* Keanu shouted, dropping to his knees beside him. His hands shook as he checked for signs of life. Hansin's amber-brown eyes were shut, his expression serene yet unnaturally still, as if caught in an endless dream.

Panic surged through Keanu, but it was entwined with a flicker of something darker—resentment, a long-buried seed that had taken root over the years. Hansin was their mother's favorite, the golden boy, while Keanu bore the weight of responsibility without the warmth of her approval. Still, all of that paled now. Keanu pushed his bitterness aside, lifting Hansin into his arms and carrying him home, his legs trembling under the dual burdens of fear and guilt.

Bursting through the front door, Keanu's voice cracked with urgency as he called for their mother. Her face turned ashen at the sight of Hansin's limp form, and together they rushed him to the hospital. The drive felt like an eternity, and the sterile hospital walls offered little comfort. His mother and brother watched as doctors worked tirelessly, their faces grave. Every tick of the clock seemed to deepen the chasm of uncertainty.

Hours passed in agonizing silence. Keanu paced the waiting room, torn between the gnawing fear of losing his brother and the guilt over his own conflicted feelings. Hansin's vulnerability in that moment stripped away the barriers Keanu had built over the years, leaving raw, unfiltered emotions.

Beneath his resentment was a fierce love, one that prayed silently to the Divine for Hansin's recovery.

Finally, the doctor emerged, his expression grim. *"Your son has fallen into a deep coma,"* he said softly. *"We don't know when—or if—he'll wake up."*

Their mother clung to Keanu, her tears soaking into his shirt. In that moment, the weight of being the eldest pressed heavily on his shoulders. Keanu realized the depth of his mother's love for both her sons, even if it hadn't always felt equal. This wasn't the time for petty grievances.

As the hospital grew quiet with the onset of night, Hansin's mother, trembling with emotion, reached for her phone. *"Mother,"* she said through a choked sob when her mother answered. *"It's Hansin… he's in a coma. The doctors don't know what to do."*

Her mother—the matriarch, keeper of wisdom, and guide of their family—listened intently. She assured her daughter that she would come as soon as possible, her voice steady and filled with an ancient strength. *"Hold on to your faith,"* she urged. *"The Divine works in ways we cannot see."*

Little did they know, Hansin was not lost to the void. His spirit had been drawn into a realm beyond mortal comprehension, a place where light and darkness clashed, and faith was not merely a belief but a weapon. There, the Divine's presence was tangible, guiding him toward a destiny he could not yet understand.

As dawn approached, a sliver of hope pierced through the heavy veil of despair. Keanu sat by Hansin's bedside, his head bowed in silent prayer. The resentment that once clouded his heart began to fade, replaced by a newfound resolve. Whatever the days ahead held, they would face them together—as brothers, as a family, and as believers in the Divine's greater plan.

The stage was set for a journey that would test their courage, their love, and their trust in the unseen hand of the Divine.

***

In the ethereal depths of the spirit realm, Hansin moved cautiously, his every step guided by Yuppi, the radiant spirit fox who had remained steadfast by his side. The atmosphere shimmered with divine hues—golden streams of light interwoven with lavender and sapphire mists, a testament to the realm's sacred beauty and the Creator's infinite artistry. Here, time felt fluid, and Hansin could sense the realm's pulse, a rhythmic echo of a world balanced delicately between light and shadow.

As they journeyed deeper, Yuppi led Hansin to an enclave hidden beneath an ancient, towering tree whose roots radiated with faint celestial energy. Waiting within were a group of weary yet resolute allies—beings once revered as mighty guardians of the Astral plane. These guardians, now shadows of their former glory, had been forced into hiding during Jezebell's dark reign. Their luminous auras had dimmed, yet their spirits bore traces of unyielding faith.

The guardians' solemn gazes met Hansin's, their expressions laced with equal parts hope and caution. *"You bear the mark of the Astral Guardian,"* one spoke, his voice carrying the weight of centuries. *"But beware. Jezebell's gaze pierces beyond the veil, and her power thrives in the void left by fear and despair."*

Yuppi's crystalline voice chimed in, *"Jezebell is a usurper of order, a disruptor of Yahweh's design. She preys on weakness, yet she fears the light of the Spirit."* Hansin absorbed their warnings, the enormity of his mission settling like a storm in his chest. He was not just lost in a strange world; he had stepped into a divine battlefield where his choices would ripple across realms.

With Yuppi's wisdom as his guide, Hansin attempted to phase back into the physical world. Standing unseen beside his family, he watched his mother weep at his bedside, her whispered prayers resonating like a melody of faith. His brother Keanu sat rigid, guilt and love warring within him. Hansin reached out, desperate to touch them, but his hand passed through like mist. A pang of loneliness struck his heart.

"Why can't I return? Why can't I touch them?" he asked Yuppi, frustration simmering beneath his words.

"You are tethered to this realm for a purpose," Yuppi explained patiently. *"Before you can walk freely between realms, you must seek the wisdom of the expired—guardians who served before you. Their strength and knowledge were given by Yahweh, and through them, you will understand your own calling."*

Yuppi's voice grew somber as he continued. *"But beware, Hansin. While you walk in the Spirit, your physical form lies unguarded. Without a Radiant Overseer to protect you, the forces of darkness can seep into the void and wreak havoc."*

Hansin's chest tightened at the mention of a Radiant Overseer. He had read of them in the sacred texts—beings chosen to anchor guardians in the physical realm, bound by a holy covenant. *"How do I find one?"* he asked.

"You do not find them," Yuppi replied with a knowing glance. *"The Creator appoints them, as He has appointed you. Trust His timing. Seek His will."*

Steeling himself, Hansin stepped forward, his resolve unwavering despite the weight pressing on his shoulders. His path was clear—he would journey to the realm of the expired, a sanctified domain where the echoes of ancient guardians dwelled. There, amidst celestial archives of memory and power, he would uncover the truths of his lineage and his connection to the Creator's purpose.

But the road would not be easy. As Yuppi led him toward the portal that shimmered in the distance, Hansin felt the encroaching chill of Jezebell's influence. Whispers, malevolent and invasive, licked at the edges of his mind, promising fear and failure. He stopped, clasping his hands together in prayer.

"Yahweh, my Redeemer, my Rock, grant me the strength to walk Your path. Guard my mind from the enemy and my heart from despair. Lead me, for I cannot do this without You."

A gentle warmth enveloped him, dispelling the shadows that had begun to gather. Yuppi tilted his head approvingly. *"Never forget, Hansin. It is in surrender to the Divine that true strength is found."*

With renewed faith, Hansin stepped into the unknown, ready to embrace his destiny. For though he was but one soul, his faith was anchored in the One who held dominion over all realms. And so, the young Astral Guardian began his sacred journey, not for his own glory, but to restore balance and reflect the Creator's light into the encroaching darkness.

Chapter 2: Forging Bonds

The moment Hansin stepped through the portal into the realm of the expired, the world around him shifted. The chaotic mists of the spirit realm faded, and he found himself in a serene, ethereal space where time seemed to move differently—slower, more deliberate, as though the very air was infused with ancient wisdom.

The ground beneath his feet was soft, almost fluid, as though it were made of stars and stardust, ever-shifting yet grounding. The landscape stretched far and wide, with vast skies swirling in hues of gold, silver, and soft purple. In the distance, towering structures—ancient temples, monuments to past Astral guardians—loomed like forgotten giants, their forms illuminated by an unearthly glow.

Yuppi's voice echoed in Hansin's mind one last time as the fox remained in the spirit realm, the divide between the two worlds closing behind him.

"Remember, Hansin, this is a place of rest for those who have walked the path before you. They will not speak to you in the way you're used to, but their presence will guide you. You must be prepared to listen with more than your ears. Trust in what you feel."

Hansin stood still for a moment, absorbing the vastness of the place. It was quiet—eerily so—yet there was a hum beneath the surface, an energy that seemed to beckon him deeper into the heart of the realm. Without another word, he began to walk forward, his heart both heavy with responsibility and light with the unspoken potential he felt in the air.

As Hansin journeyed, the realm began to reveal itself to him in fragments. Shadows of past guardians appeared at the periphery of his vision—faint but distinct, like shimmering outlines of great warriors who had once stood guard over the balance between worlds. Each figure was bound to a particular element, and as Hansin passed, he could feel their gaze on him, like the weight of their collective history pressing gently upon his soul.

He came upon a large circular plaza at the center of the realm, where several guardians—ancient and glowing with celestial energy—stood in a perfect ring. Their eyes were closed, their bodies still, as though they were in eternal meditation, yet Hansin could feel their power stirring the very air around him.

A tall figure, dressed in robes woven from the essence of stars, stepped forward. He was the first to open his eyes, which burned with the intensity of a thousand suns. His voice, when he spoke, was like a distant thunderclap, full of both warmth and weight.

"You have come seeking guidance, young one," he said, his voice resonating deep within Hansin's chest. *"But know this: here in the realm of the expired, you will find no easy answers. We are not here to teach you how to wield your power. We are here to show you the path, and the path is yours to walk."*

Hansin nodded, swallowing the lump in his throat. He wasn't sure what he had expected, but it certainly wasn't this. The enormity of the responsibility that lay before him seemed almost impossible to bear, yet there was something undeniably compelling about the guardians' presence. They had walked this road before, and now, it was his turn.

The guardian continued, his gaze unwavering. *"To truly understand the abilities of the Radiant Overseers and the strength within you, you must first understand the essence of the elements you are destined to command. We will show you their power, but you must forge your own connection with them. You must listen to the Divine."*

Hansin's chest tightened at the mention of the Divine. He had only felt His presence briefly, a faint pull in the back of his mind, but here, in this place, it seemed to saturate everything—every guardian, every breath of air.

As Hansin stood before the ancient guardian, still processing the vastness of the realm and the gravity of his journey, the guardian's gaze softened, and he nodded as if reading Hansin's unspoken thoughts.

"Before we begin your training, young one, you must understand the history that binds you to this moment," the guardian's voice boomed softly. *"You are not merely a vessel for power. You are the bridge between the realms—between the physical and the spirit."*

The guardian paused, allowing the weight of his words to settle into Hansin's heart. Then, slowly, he began to weave a tale that resonated deep within Hansin's soul.

"The Radiant Overseers are beings of unimaginable power, born of both light and shadow. They were the original protectors of the Astral realm, tasked with maintaining balance between life and death, light and dark, physical and spiritual. They are the keepers of the

elements—each one embodying an aspect of nature: Earth, Fire, Water, Air, and Light."

Hansin listened intently, but the vastness of what the guardian was saying overwhelmed him. These overseers were not just figures of legend—they were real, tangible forces tied to his very existence.

"But these overseers do not simply control the elements," the guardian continued. *"They are bound to their chosen Astral guardians. It is through this sacred bond that they empower the guardians, guiding them to fulfill their roles. In turn, the guardians protect the balance, keeping the realms aligned and the forces of darkness at bay."*

Hansin nodded, his mind trying to absorb this crucial information. The Radiant Overseers, then, were his allies, but their bond with him meant that he could never truly walk alone. But there was something else, something deeper, that the guardian's eyes hinted at as he spoke.

"There is another truth you must understand, Hansin," the guardian's voice darkened. *"The bond between a guardian and their Radiant Overseer is sacred and unbreakable. But it is also a weakness. You, as an Astral guardian, are tethered to the physical realm through your overseer. As long as you remain unconscious, as you are now, your physical body is vulnerable—unprotected without an overseer."*

Hansin's heart quickened, a sudden fear creeping into his chest.

"And there are those in the physical realm who would use this weakness to their advantage."

The guardian's words hung heavily in the air. Hansin could feel the weight of them deep in his bones. He opened his mouth to speak, but before he could ask, the guardian's gaze turned cold and solemn.

"Jezebell, the malevolent overlord who now rules over much of the spirit realm, has long sought to escape her prison. She has sensed your presence, Hansin, your essence—a potential threat she thought had vanished long ago."

The guardian paused, his eyes narrowing with a dark intensity.

"Jezebell's dark forces have already been dispatched to the physical realm. They seek you, Hansin, and they will stop at nothing to trap you. Once they find you, they will attempt to return you to her, where she will corrupt your bond with your Radiant Overseer and use you as a weapon to escape the spirit realm

and dominate both realms—physical and spiritual."

Hansin's stomach dropped at the thought of being used as a pawn in Jezebell's twisted game. He had come here seeking knowledge, hoping to learn how to protect both the realms and those he loved, but now he realized the true danger of his journey. It wasn't just about learning his powers—it was about surviving the forces that wanted to control them.

The guardian's voice softened, but there was an edge of urgency in his tone.

"You must understand the danger you face, Hansin. The Radiant Overseers are not invincible, nor are they the sole force that protects you. Your bond with them can be broken by the darkness—by manipulation, by fear, and by those who seek to twist your will. You are vulnerable in your current state, and

while you are in the realm of the expired, your body lies unprotected in the physical realm, awaiting the dark forces to close in."

Hansin's mind raced. Jezebell was already aware of him, and her forces were likely closing in. His journey into the realm of the expired had been his only chance to learn and grow, but now it had become a race against time. He needed to hurry—to not only prepare himself but also to find a way to protect his body and stop Jezebell's forces from succeeding.

"But I will not leave you to face this alone," the guardian said, stepping closer. *"We will teach you how to harness your power, but the greatest strength you will need is faith—faith in the Divine and the bond between you and your overseer, and faith in the light*

that will guide you through the darkest of times."

Hansin felt a surge of determination rise within him. He could not allow Jezebell's darkness to consume both realms. With every fiber of his being, he knew that he had to succeed—not just for his own sake but for the future of all worlds.

"What must I do?" Hansin asked, his voice steady despite the fear that still churned within him.

The guardian nodded, his eyes glowing with ancient wisdom.

"You must first learn to connect with the elements, Hansin. You must understand the essence of each one—Earth, Fire, Water, Air, and Light—and learn to wield them with the power and wisdom of your ancestors. Only then will you be ready to face the darkness that comes for you."

Hansin's training in the realm of the expired began with what seemed like a simple exercise but proved to be far more complex. The guardian, who had introduced himself as Elrin, led Hansin to the center of a great, still lake that shimmered like silver beneath the twilight of the realm. The surface of the water rippled gently, as though it was alive.

"To begin," Elrin spoke, *"you must learn to connect with the elements, as they are the foundation of your power. The spirits of the expired guardians are the keepers of this knowledge, and it is through them that you will forge your path."*

At first, Hansin's attempts were clumsy. He stood with his arms extended over the water, trying to summon the energy of the element, but nothing happened. His mind raced as he concentrated, remembering the sense of magic he'd felt in the Astral realm but now felt distant and inaccessible.

"The elements do not respond to force," Elrin explained patiently, watching Hansin's frustration rise. *"They are not to be controlled by sheer will. They are part of you, Hansin. You must invite them, not demand them. You must become one with them, feel their essence in your heart and soul. Only then will they flow through you."*

With Elrin's guidance, Hansin focused inward, seeking a deeper connection with his surroundings. Slowly, his breathing evened, and the air around him seemed to grow heavier with energy. He closed his eyes and extended his senses, feeling the pulse of the wind as it whispered through the trees, the steady grounding pull of the earth beneath him, and the vibrant energy of the water beneath his feet.

Then, something shifted. He felt a warm glow within him, a quiet hum of energy that began to resonate with the world around him. Slowly, water began to rise from the lake's surface, forming delicate spirals and arcs in the air.

"Good," Elrin said, his voice full of approval. *"This is just the beginning, but you are already beginning to understand the flow of energy."*

Hansin felt a surge of hope. Though it was only a small display of power, he realized that he could learn this—he could control it.

For the next few hours, Hansin's training continued. Elrin taught him to manipulate the wind, sending gusts swirling around him. He connected with the earth, sensing its vast power as he summoned small tremors beneath his feet. He practiced molding fire, and even light, which filled him with a warmth that felt like the embrace of the sun. But each lesson was incomplete. No matter how much he learned, Hansin could not yet feel the full depth of the connection that would bind him to his Radiant Overseer. This connection, Elrin explained, would come when the time was right. For now, he needed to focus on the elements, on mastering them in small steps.

Meanwhile, in the shadowy corners of the spirit realm, Jezebell sat upon a darkened throne, her cold eyes glinting with malice. Her thoughts were elsewhere, her attention drawn to an energy she had never felt before—an unfamiliar essence that rippled across the astral plains. She leaned forward, her sharp gaze narrowing.

"It cannot be," Jezebell murmured to herself. *"The Astral Guardians were thought to be no more. Yet this energy—this presence—feels like one of them. But how?"*

She tapped a finger against the arm of her throne, her mind racing with possibilities. If an Astral Guardian had indeed returned, it would be a threat—perhaps the greatest threat to her dominion over both realms. She could not afford to let such a force grow unchecked.

Jezebell called out with a chilling command, summoning her Phantom Legionnaires—an army of ghostly warriors bound to her will. As they materialized before her, their forms flickering like shadows, she addressed them with urgency.

"Find the source of this energy," Jezebell commanded. *"Seek out the being who*

dares to wield the power of the Astral Guardians. Trap them before they fully awaken. Bring them to me. I will not allow any force to stand in my way as I prepare to escape this realm and dominate both worlds."

The legionnaires bowed without a word, their spectral forms disappearing into the mists of the spirit realm, their mission clear.

Back in the physical realm, Hansin's family sat by his side in the hospital, anxiety written on their faces. His grandmother, a woman deeply attuned to the unseen forces that surrounded them, sat in quiet contemplation. Her aged eyes, though clouded with age, seemed to see beyond the physical world.

"Something is wrong," she murmured, her voice low. *"I can feel it. The*

shadows grow thicker around him. We cannot stay here."

Her daughter, Hansin's mother, looked at her in confusion. *"What do you mean, Mom? The doctors say there's nothing more we can do but wait."*

"No," the grandmother insisted, her voice hardening with conviction. *"There is a force at work here—something dark. We must move him to a sacred ground, a place where his energy can be shielded."*

The grandmother stood, her frailty forgotten in the face of the deep concern etched on her face. She paced for a moment, her fingers brushing over the family heirlooms that adorned the room—a few old talismans of protection. Her mind already made up, she turned to Hansin's mother.

"We must take him to the sacred ground of the Ancients. It is protected from the forces that would seek to harm him, and it is the only place where he can remain safe for now."

"The Ancients…?" Hansin's mother whispered, fear creeping into her voice. *"But that place… it is not easy to reach."*

The grandmother nodded grimly. *"We must go there now. Before it's too late."*

In the sterile, dimly lit hospital room, the weight of silence hung heavy as Hansin's mother and grandmother stood over his unconscious form. The machines beeped rhythmically, but no one spoke, their minds racing with their own thoughts. Keanu, Hansin's older brother, stood at the window, his arms crossed tightly across his chest. He watched the nurses pass by outside but was not really seeing them. His mind was consumed by the unsettling reality of his brother's coma.

"What's going on?" Keanu finally burst out, his voice filled with frustration. *"Why are we acting like this is all some kind of secret? You've kept things from me—both of you! What is this sacred ground you're talking about? Why can't you just tell me what's really going on?"*

His mother, who had been standing by Hansin's side, turned to him, her face clouded with worry. *"Keanu, this isn't the time. We'll explain everything later. Right now, we need to focus on getting Hansin somewhere safe."*

Keanu shook his head, growing more exasperated. *"Safe? From what? You're not telling me what's really happening. What are you hiding? Why did we have to rush him here in the first place? And why have you kept me in the dark for so long?"*

His grandmother, who had been silently observing the scene, sighed heavily. She had been expecting this moment, knowing that Keanu would eventually grow frustrated with the secrecy that had been maintained around Hansin's situation. She walked slowly toward him, her voice calm and steady, despite the urgency of the moment.

"Keanu, I understand your frustration," she said softly. *"But there is much you don't know—things we've kept from you for your protection. We did it because we feared that you might be led astray. But now is not the time for explanations. There is a far greater danger, and we must focus on that first."*

Keanu's eyes narrowed as he stepped closer to her, his voice rising in anger. *"What danger? And why couldn't you trust me? I'm your son! I deserve to know what's going on!"*

The grandmother's gaze softened, and she placed a hand on his shoulder. *"Because you were not ready to understand, Keanu. And because we feared the truth might pull you away from the path you are meant to follow. Hansin... is different. He is a guardian, Keanu. He is destined for something far greater than you or I could ever comprehend. The danger that surrounds him now is not just of this world. And if we do not act quickly, that danger could consume him... and us all."*

Keanu blinked, his confusion deepening. *"A guardian? What do you mean? I don't understand. How is that even possible?"*

The grandmother's expression grew distant, her eyes clouded with memories of the past. She sighed again, her faith unwavering even in the face of their uncertainty. *"I will explain, Keanu. But not here. Not now. Once Hansin is safe, once we have him in a place of protection, then I will tell you everything."*

Her tone left no room for argument, and Keanu, though still filled with questions, fell silent. His mother stepped forward, touching his arm gently. *"We need to leave here now. If we wait too long, they'll never let us take him. You don't understand, Keanu, but there's no time to explain everything just yet."*

Keanu's frustration simmered beneath the surface, but his gaze shifted to Hansin, his younger brother, lying so still and vulnerable in the hospital bed. He swallowed hard, his anger giving way to concern for Hansin's well-being yet a tinge of jealousy at the mention of his younger brother being a guardian and not him.

"So, what do we do now?" Keanu asked, his voice lower, tinged with reluctance.

The grandmother turned toward the door, her voice unwavering as she spoke. *"We get him out of here. We take him to the sacred ground. It is our only option. The place will shield him from the dangers that are already closing in on him. But we cannot do this without your help, Keanu."*

Keanu hesitated, his eyes flickering between his grandmother and his unconscious brother. It was clear that something extraordinary was happening, something that no one was fully explaining. But one thing was certain: Hansin's safety was at the center of it all.

"I don't know what's going on," Keanu said, his voice quiet now. *"But I'll help. I'll do whatever it takes to get him out of here."*

The grandmother nodded, a glint of approval in her eyes. *"Good. Trust in the*

Divine will, Keanu. Trust that this path we walk is the one we are meant to follow. And you will come to understand everything in time."

With that, the family gathered their things. They would move quickly and quietly, but they had to be careful. The hospital staff would never let them leave without question, especially with Hansin in such a critical state. They would need to craft a plan—one that would allow them to get Hansin to the sacred ground without attracting attention.

Chapter 3: Family Legacy

Hansin's breath caught in his chest as his great-grandmother sat across from him, her frail but steady hands gripping her cane. The sacred grounds, a place of spiritual power and deep ancestral ties, hummed with an energy that resonated through Hansin's very being. He had shifted back into the physical realm from the expanse of the spirit world, a process that felt like an awakening, a return to a reality where everything—his family, his legacy, and his mission—was more urgent than ever.

After embracing his family, his grandmother spoke with urgency. *"Now that you're safely here, Hansin, it's time you learned the truth."* His great-grandmother's voice, ancient yet sharp, cut through the stillness of the air.

Hansin nodded, a sense of anticipation rising in him. His heart raced with both excitement and apprehension. He had long suspected there was more to his family's history than what he had been told, but nothing had prepared him for the weight of the revelations his great-grandmother was about to share.

"Listen well, Hansin, for the tale I am about to tell you is the story of our bloodline and the sacred duty we have upheld for generations."

With those words, the room seemed to shift, the past and present blending together as his great-grandmother began her tale.

"Our ancestors were not always who you know us to be. The Jasper tribe, as you know it, began long ago, in a time when the physical realm and the Astral realm were one, a seamless entity. The first of our line, a visionary blessed with

astral sight, became the first Astral guardian—chosen not by chance, but by divine will.”

Hansin closed his eyes briefly, imagining the scenes unfolding in his mind: warriors from ancient times standing at the borders between realms, defending a world unknown to most.

“This ancestor of ours,” his great-grandmother continued, *“was the first to perceive the unseen energies of the Astral realm. With this gift came immense responsibility. He was entrusted with maintaining the balance between the two worlds, to guard against those who would seek to tear the veil that separated them.”*

Hansin felt a rush of awe as the magnitude of his family's history settled on him. The power of astral sight, the duty of guardianship—these were his roots. He had felt it within himself, a deep connection to something far greater than his own life.

But as his great-grandmother's voice deepened with a sorrowful undertone, the story took a darker turn.

"Our bloodline has not been without struggle, Hansin. We have faced darkness, and we have paid a heavy price. Wars have been fought, sacrifices made, and great losses endured. The forces we have battled—forces that threaten the very existence of both realms—are relentless."

Hansin felt a cold shiver trace down his spine as the weight of those words settled in. His mind flashed back to the dreamlike visions he had experienced in the spirit realm, the sense that something—someone—was closing in on him.

"And now," his great-grandmother's voice became resolute, her gaze piercing through him, *"the time has come for you to fulfill your destiny as the next Astral guardian of the Jasper tribe. You, Hansin, are the one who will stand between the realms and the coming storm."*

The words struck Hansin like a bolt of lightning. His heart swelled with determination, and yet, fear lingered on the edges of his thoughts. Was he truly ready for this burden? For the fight his ancestors had fought?

"You carry the legacy of those who came before you, Hansin," his great-grandmother's words softened, but were no less powerful. *"The strength of our tribe, the wisdom of our bloodline, and the guidance of the Divine and our ancestors will be with you. But this is a*

journey you must walk alone, at least in the beginning."

Hansin nodded, his resolve hardening. He had no choice but to accept the responsibility placed before him. Yet, as the words hung in the air, a new question emerged.

"What of Jezebell?" Hansin asked, the name slipping from his lips like a whispered curse.

At the mention of the name, his great-grandmother's face darkened. Her eyes clouded with a mixture of fear and solemnity.

"Jezebell..." she muttered, her voice barely a whisper. *"She is the greatest threat we have ever faced. A malevolent being, one who seeks to tear down the veil between realms and escape into the physical world. She has long been a shadow, waiting for a moment of*

57

weakness, a time when the balance will shift in her favor. And now, with your awakening, Hansin, she senses that moment is near."

Hansin's stomach churned as he absorbed the gravity of her words. Jezebell was not just an adversary; she was a force of darkness, a harbinger of chaos, and she was coming for him.

"We must prepare," his great-grandmother said, her voice firm once more. *"The Radiant Overseers, the ancient protectors of the Astral Guardians, are the key to defeating Jezebell. They are not simply beings of strength; they are linked to the Divine. Only with them can we hope to stand against the darkness."*

Hansin felt the weight of her words settle upon him. He could feel the pull of something greater than himself, something divine, calling him to fulfill his role, to be more than just the heir to the Jasper tribe—he was a beacon, a vessel for something sacred. His heart stirred with a fire of determination, but a part of him felt overwhelmed by the enormity of the task ahead.

As his great-grandmother finished speaking, Hansin sat in contemplative silence, his mind spinning with the knowledge that he was not only facing an ancient evil but also that his journey had just begun. The path to finding the Radiant Overseers, the mysterious and powerful beings who could guide him and protect his body during his training in the spirit realm, felt both perilous and urgent.

Then, the quiet was broken by Keanu's voice, tinged with frustration and confusion.

"And what about me, huh? You're just going to leave me out of all this?" Keanu

stood at the doorway, arms crossed, his expression a mix of anger and hurt. He had been listening to the conversation but had been silent until now.

Hansin turned to look at him, sensing the tension building in his cousin. The divine guidance that had stirred within him faltered for a moment. Hansin knew that Keanu had never been told the full truth about their bloodline and had never felt the weight of their legacy. The secrecy had protected him, and yet now, it seemed to breed resentment.

"Keanu, this is not your fight, it's not even mine alone, it is a calling of the Divine," Hansin began, trying to explain gently. *"You don't understand—this is about something bigger than us. It's about the balance of both realms, and I... I'm the one chosen to bear this burden. Our family... has protected this legacy for generations."*

But Keanu wasn't listening. His jaw clenched, and a bitter laugh escaped him. *"So you're telling me I've been kept in the dark all these years, just so you could play the hero? You think just because you're the 'chosen one' that you get all the answers? You don't even know what you're facing yet!"*

The words stung, and Hansin felt a pang of guilt. Keanu had always been close to him, but this sudden shift in his attitude was jarring. It wasn't just confusion Keanu was feeling—it was jealousy, a deep-rooted frustration that Hansin had been entrusted with something Keanu felt he was equally deserving of.

Hansin's great-grandmother, sensing the rising tension, spoke with quiet authority, her voice cutting through the emotions swirling in the room.

"Keanu, your time will come," she said, her gaze sharp and unwavering. *"Do not*

let jealousy cloud your purpose. The Divine will will unfold in its own time, and all will be revealed when it is meant to be. You must trust in this, just as Hansin must trust in his own path. He needs your support not your division, united we stand."

Keanu's frustration simmered, but he swallowed his words and turned away, pacing angrily. The divine wisdom of his great-grandmother settled in his heart, but his mind still churned with the unfairness of the situation.

Meanwhile, Hansin, though inwardly shaken, felt a sense of resolve rising within him. He knew the Divine had called him, and he had to rise above the darkness that loomed not only in the physical realm but also within the hearts of those closest to him.

That night, Hansin lay on his makeshift bed, restless but reflective. His thoughts turned inward, remembering the lessons he had learned in the realm of the expired. He closed his eyes, letting the memories wash over him—the shimmering gates of the celestial realm, the ancient Astral guardians who had imparted wisdom to him, and the sense of awe he had felt in the presence of beings who were both mentors and ancestors.

"I must be ready," he whispered to himself, his breath steadying. *"For both the Radiant Overseers and the darkness Jezebell will bring."*

With those words, Hansin bowed his head, lifting his heart to the Divine. He whispered a prayer, hoping that his words would reach beyond the physical realm.

"Divine Creator, Source of all power, guide me in this journey. Grant me the strength to protect the bond between the

realms, the wisdom to guard the Overseers, and the courage to stand against the darkness that seeks to tear it all asunder. Fill my heart with unwavering trust in Your will, and let Your light guide my every step. Protect my family and all those who fight for balance. Let me walk in the footsteps of my ancestors, and may Your divine will be done in me, through me, and for the realms."

Hansin sat in silence for a long moment, his mind at peace, though the weight of his destiny still pressed heavily upon him. With the prayer, the stirring of the Divine settled within him, and he felt a renewed sense of purpose—knowing that he was not alone, and that the strength of the heavens themselves would guide him through the trials to come.

The next morning, as Hansin began to share his experiences with his family, Keanu, despite his lingering bitterness, remained attentive. He listened intently as Hansin spoke of the incredible power he had begun to learn to harness. Hansin described the various forms of astral energy he had encountered, his mind and spirit stretching beyond their limits. He recounted the ancient training methods he had witnessed, the powers of telekinesis and elemental control that had been passed down through the ages. But even as Hansin spoke with growing excitement, Keanu's jealousy festered, twisting his admiration for Hansin's experiences into something darker.

"And what of the Radiant Overseers?" Keanu asked, his tone laced with skepticism. *"You speak of these beings like they're some kind of celestial saviors, but what about the real fight?*

What if the Overseers don't show up in time?"

Hansin paused, meeting Keanu's eyes. *"We're not fighting alone,"* Hansin replied, his voice steady. *"The Divine will guide us, but we must be strong, too. That's what I learned. Strength comes from within, from the connection to the Astral realm and our bloodline."*

Keanu snorted but said nothing more. The bitterness was still there, unspoken, simmering beneath the surface.

As the family gathered to discuss their next steps, Hansin's great-grandmother felt a sense of urgency rise in her. She turned her attention back to Hansin, her expression shifting to one of deep contemplation.

"We cannot delay any longer," she said, her eyes narrowing with determination. *"Your Radiant Overseer must be found,*

and soon. Jezebell's forces are already moving, and we cannot afford to take chances. Every moment we waste brings the threat closer."

Hansin nodded, feeling the weight of the Divine calling pressing upon him. The journey ahead would not be easy, and the forces of darkness were closing in, but he was ready. His heart swelled with purpose, bolstered by the knowledge that his family stood beside him, even if their paths were still uncertain.

"I understand, Grandmother," Hansin said quietly, his gaze unwavering. *"But how will we find her? If she's the last of the Radiant Overseers, how can we be sure she's the one who will help me?"*

His great-grandmother's expression softened. She placed a hand on his shoulder, the weight of her centuries of wisdom pressing into him like a quiet reassurance.

"The Divine will guide us, Hansin. The Overseer will find you when the time is right. But we must move swiftly. There is no time to waste. Jezebell will not rest, and neither can we."

Hansin inhaled deeply, centering himself. His heart, though burdened, felt a flicker of hope stir within it. He was not alone in this fight; the Divine was with him, and his family would see him through.

The air in the room grew heavy with the unspoken urgency, as everyone prepared to embark on the next phase of their journey.

"Let us pray," Hansin said, closing his eyes and lifting his voice in quiet reverence.

"Divine One, we seek Your guidance in this time of peril. We are but vessels in Your hands, and we ask for Your

*wisdom and protection. Guide us to the
Radiant Overseer, that we may fulfill the
sacred duty You have laid before me.
Strengthen my heart, and protect those I
hold dear. We place our trust in You,
knowing You will lead us in this fight
against the darkness. May Your will be
done. In Your holy name, Amen."*

As Hansin finished, a calmness settled
over the room, the Divine's presence felt
in the stillness that followed. It was as if
a shield of peace had been placed
around them, fortifying their resolve.

Hansin shared the knowledge he had
gained in the realm of the expired, his
family listened with a mix of awe and
growing concern. His
great-grandmother, who had always
been the steady pillar of their tribe,
nodded gravely.

*"You've seen the power that resides in
the Astral realm, Hansin, but remember,*

it is not just your own strength that will carry you forward. It is the protection of the Radiant Overseers that will ensure you can shift safely between realms, and that bond is what keeps the line between the physical and Astral realms intact."

Hansin nodded, but a tinge of doubt lingered in his heart. *"So, it's not just my power I need to worry about. The Overseers... they're just as important, but they could be corrupted if they fall into the wrong hands, couldn't they?"* He looked to his great-grandmother for confirmation, his voice low with concern.

His great-grandmother's expression grew solemn. *"Yes, Hansin. The bond between an Astral Guardian and their Overseer is sacred. It keeps us safe when we shift. But if the Overseer is corrupted, it would not only endanger the Guardian but also threaten the balance between the realms themselves. That is why we must be cautious. Jezebell's forces will seek to manipulate the Radiant Overseers and twist them to their will."*

As Hansin pondered her words, a shadow of doubt passed over his face, and Keanu's voice cut through the silence once more, tinged with an edge of jealousy.

"And what makes you think you can handle all this? What makes you so sure you can control this power? You talk about the Overseers like they're your saviors, but what if you can't protect them?"

Hansin met his brother's eyes, a flicker of understanding crossing his mind. Keanu's jealousy had shifted into something darker, but Hansin knew that this was more than just envy—it was fear. Keanu feared being left behind, fearing that Hansin, the chosen one, would succeed while he remained in the shadows.

But Hansin remained calm, trying to keep his emotions in check. *"It's not about controlling them, Keanu. It's about trust. The Radiant Overseer will protect me while I am in the spirit realm, but I must protect them in turn. It is a bond, a sacred connection."*

Keanu huffed, his arms crossed over his chest. *"So, you're telling me the fate of the realms is resting on these Overseers and your ability to not mess things up? That's a lot of pressure, Hansin."*

Hansin felt the weight of his brother's words, but he didn't let them distract him. He knew what was at stake. The Radiant Overseers were not invincible, and their bond with the Astral Guardians could be a double-edged sword. If

Jezebell's forces corrupted an Overseer, it would spell disaster for both realms.

His great-grandmother, sensing the tension between the brothers, spoke softly, her voice a calm and guiding force led by the Divine. *"The truth, Keanu, is that we all have our roles to play. Hansin's destiny is set, but your path, though different, is no less important. You must trust in the Divine will, even if it is not immediately clear."*

Hansin felt the stirring of the Divine once more, the connection to something greater than himself. It was a power that could not be denied, and it surged through him as he spoke, his voice steady and filled with conviction.

"The Radiant Overseers are essential, Keanu. Without them, my powers could be unstable. And if they are corrupted, the entire balance of the realms will

collapse. That's why we must find them—before Jezebell does."

Keanu fell silent, but Hansin could see the flicker of doubt in his eyes. For now, Hansin would continue to walk his path, but the road ahead was uncertain, fraught with dangers that could tear apart even the closest of bonds. The Radiant Overseers were a necessary force, but they were not invulnerable, and their potential for corruption was a threat that loomed large.

As the family gathered their belongings and prepared for the next phase of their journey, Hansin knew that his connection to the Astral realm—and the Overseers—would be tested. He had to learn not just to harness the power within him, but to protect it, and protect the overseers who would ensure his safety during his shifts.

"The Radiant Overseers are the key to our survival," Hansin thought as he gazed out into the horizon. *"Without them, there is no balance. But I cannot let them be corrupted. I cannot fail."*

The Divine stirred within him, and for the first time, Hansin fully understood the magnitude of his role. His destiny as the Astral Guardian was intertwined with the fate of both realms, and the journey to find the Radiant Overseers would not be an easy one. But with his great-grandmother's wisdom and his family's support, Hansin knew that he could not falter.

The family set out on their quest to find the Radiant Overseers, but as the journey progressed, the threat of Jezebell loomed ever closer, and Hansin's was tested in ways he had never imagined. His bond with the Overseer would prove to be the greatest challenge of all, as the balance between the realms hung in the balance, waiting for the Astral Guardians to rise and defend all they had sworn to protect.

Chapter 4: Balancing Acts

The morning light filtered through the trees, casting long shadows over the group as they prepared for the journey ahead. Hansin's family had gathered, each of them tense with the weight of the task at hand. They were on their way to find the Radiant Overseer, the only remaining one of her kind in the physical realm, and yet, Hansin knew the journey ahead would not be an easy one. The overseer they sought would not be someone easy to persuade, someone willing to fall into the divine role she had been chosen for.

"We cannot delay any longer," his great-grandmother said, her voice cutting through the air like a blade. She was the one who had guided them thus far, leading them in their quest to find Tuwa. *"The Divine has chosen her for a reason. We must make her see that."*

Hansin nodded, his heart heavy with the knowledge that this part of the journey would be the most difficult yet. Tuwa, the Radiant Overseer, was not the calm, wise protector they had imagined as revealed to by his grandmother. She was a rebellious, headstrong teenager—someone who had rejected her divine destiny for so long that even the idea of it had become something she resented.

The family moved in silence, the weight of their purpose hanging in the air. Hansin's thoughts, however, were anything but silent. He thought of the Overseer they were about to find—Tuwa—and of what lay ahead. She was a mystery to him, a key part of his journey yet so far removed from the image he had in his mind.

As the group finally arrived at the place where Tuwa was said to be, Hansin's heart raced. It was a small, almost inconspicuous clearing, a space hidden from the world, a place where the forces of the Divine met the natural world. The ground was littered with fragments of light that shimmered underfoot, a sign that this was no ordinary place.

Tuwa was sitting cross-legged on the ground, her back turned to them. She looked like a typical rebellious teenager, her messy hair cascading around her shoulders, her posture defiant, even in the face of those who sought her out.

"You've found me," Tuwa said, her voice dripping with sarcasm as she stood slowly, turning to face them. *"What do you want?"*

Hansin stepped forward, trying to maintain his composure despite her harsh words. He knew she didn't yet understand her role, but he had to believe she would.

"You are the Radiant Overseer, Tuwa. The Divine has called you to protect me, to help me in this fight against Jezebell," Hansin said quietly, meeting her gaze. *"You are a protector, one who stands between the physical realm and the dangers that threaten it."*

Tuwa's eyes narrowed, and she crossed her arms over her chest, clearly uninterested. *"Yeah, well, I'm not interested. This whole 'chosen one' thing that everyone has been talking to me about lately? Doesn't sound like my problem."*

Hansin felt a pang of frustration but kept his voice steady. *"Tuwa, you have a purpose. We need you."*

But Tuwa was having none of it. She scoffed and turned her back to him, staring off into the distance. *"I don't need anyone. I've gotten by just fine without any of you,"* she muttered under her breath, barely audible.

Hansin felt a deep sense of responsibility for her, as if the Divine had placed her in his path for a reason. He could feel the tension between them, the distance that she had built around herself, refusing to accept the truth of her calling. Yet Hansin had been through his own struggles with accepting his role as the Astral guardian. He had to find a way to help her see that she wasn't alone in this—she didn't have to fight her destiny, not when the Divine was by her side.

"I know it's hard to believe in something bigger than yourself," Hansin said gently, his voice filled with empathy. *"I've struggled with it too. But the Divine has a plan for you, for both of us. I've felt it. And now it's your turn to trust that plan."*

Tuwa didn't respond immediately. For a long moment, she simply stared at him, her jaw clenched in irritation. Hansin wasn't sure if his words had gotten through to her, but he remained resolute. He knew the battle wasn't just about the physical fight against Jezebell—it was about helping Tuwa understand her purpose, to believe in something greater than herself, and to accept the role she had been given.

As they continued to speak, Hansin shared more of his experiences, both in the physical and the spirit realm, and how the Divine had guided him, even when he had doubted. He spoke of his training, his connection to the astral realm, and the lessons he had learned from the other Astral guardians. Slowly, as Tuwa listened to him, her defiance began to waver. There was something in his words, something steady and unshakeable, that sparked a flicker of something inside her—a curiosity, perhaps, or maybe the first hint of belief.

"So, what exactly are you trying to tell me?" Tuwa asked, her voice quieter than before. There was a shift in her tone, a slight break in her walls.

"I'm saying you're not alone in this," Hansin said. *"We don't have to fight this battle by ourselves. I've been training in the realm of the expired, learning from the guardians who have gone before us. And I believe you have the strength to do the same, to step into your role as the Radiant Overseer. You can't do it alone, but with the Divine guiding us, we will stand against Jezebell."*

For the first time, Tuwa seemed to hesitate. She looked down at her hands, almost as if contemplating the weight of what he was saying.

"And you really believe in this... this Divine? After everything you've been through?" Tuwa asked, her voice softer now, laced with a new kind of uncertainty.

Hansin met her gaze without hesitation. *"Yes. With all my heart. It's through the Divine that I've been able to come this far. And it's through the Divine that we will overcome Jezebell."*

There was a long silence between them, and Hansin could feel the shift in the air. Tuwa was no longer completely resistant, though she was still far from convinced. But he could see the seed of doubt in her mind beginning to crack, the idea of faith slowly taking root.

Slowly, her stance softened. *"Fine,"* Tuwa said reluctantly. *"I'll listen. But that doesn't mean I'm going to just roll over and accept all this... divine fate stuff."*

Hansin smiled, his heart filled with a quiet hope. He knew that this was only the beginning, but it was a start—a start that would lead them both to understanding, to strength, and ultimately to victory.

As Tuwa began to see the truth in his words, a subtle shift occurred. The faith Hansin had so steadfastly clung to began to seep into her heart as well. She began to believe, and with that belief came the unlocking of her own powers. Her light began to shine brighter, her strength growing with each step she took toward her destiny as the Radiant Overseer. She wasn't there yet, but Hansin could see it in her—the first spark of true belief.

And as her powers began to grow, so too did their bond. She was no longer just his protector—she was becoming his ally, and perhaps, in time, something more. But, there was another that had eyes for Tuwa, that would not easily back off.

***

As Hansin juggled his life between the physical realm and his responsibilities as an Astral guardian, he found himself stretched thin. The weight of his duty as a protector of both realms was heavy on his shoulders. School was becoming increasingly difficult to manage, as his focus shifted to training and growing in his powers. His academic performance began to slip, and the pressures of relationships with his friends and family only seemed to grow more complicated.

Each day, Hansin felt more disconnected from the normal life he once knew. The assignments piled up, but his mind kept drifting back to his training sessions in the realm of the expired. In that realm, the wisdom of his ancestors and the teachings of the ancient Astral guardians burned brightly in his mind. But here, in the physical world, he couldn't afford to ignore his responsibilities to his family and the world that depended on him.

As Hansin entered his meditative trance, his mind drifting deep into the spiritual realms to continue his training, Tuwa stood vigilantly by his side. Her radiant energy pulsed around her like a protective shield, a force that kept the darkness at bay while Hansin's consciousness roamed the astral planes. Her role as his Radiant Overseer was not just one of passive protection—she was actively involved in the fight against Jezebell's Phantom Legionnaires, the malevolent spirits sent to corrupt and disrupt Hansin's growth.

The air around Tuwa crackled with energy, her aura glowing in a brilliant, ethereal light. She had learned to harness the full extent of her powers, but they were still new to her, raw and untamed. Every protective ward she cast over Hansin felt like a step closer to understanding her true role in this battle. She could feel the weight of the task before her, the responsibility to protect Hansin's physical body while he trained, while also struggling with her own resistance to accepting her destiny.

As Hansin's body lay still, his mind battling the trials of the spirit realm, Tuwa felt the approach of the Phantom Legionnaires. Their presence was subtle at first—an unsettling chill in the air, the faintest whisper of dark energy. They moved like shadows, formless and terrifying, seeking any vulnerability in Hansin's aura. Their intent was clear: to disrupt his training, to weaken him, and to prevent him from fulfilling his divine calling.

Tuwa's heart beat faster as she drew upon the power within her, her hands glowing with radiant light. She raised her arms high, her energy swirling around her like a whirlwind, and with a focused gesture, she cast a brilliant shield of light around Hansin's body. The Phantom Legionnaires began to materialize, their forms twisted and horrifying, their eyes glowing with malice. They hissed and howled, trying to break through the radiant barrier Tuwa had created.

"You cannot touch him," Tuwa said fiercely, her voice steady and full of power. *"Not while I stand here."*

The phantoms screeched, recoiling from the intense light that radiated from her. Tuwa's powers as a Radiant Overseer were still in their infancy, but the raw energy she commanded was undeniable. She had spent hours in silent meditation, learning to harness the light within her, understanding how it could ward off the darkness that threatened to consume them all. As the phantoms charged forward once more, Tuwa focused her energy into a single beam of blinding light, sending it crashing into the shadows. The phantoms shrieked in agony as the light tore through their forms, forcing them to dissipate into nothingness.

Still, they returned, more determined than ever. Tuwa gritted her teeth, refusing to allow them to breach the protective barrier around Hansin. *"You will not win,"* she muttered, her voice thick with both anger and resolve. *"I will protect him."*

Each time the phantoms came closer, she met them with a strike of pure light. It wasn't just her powers she relied on—there was something else now. A deep well of unwavering faith in the Divine that sustained her, a belief that no matter how many times the phantoms returned, she would stand her ground. She could feel Hansin's presence in her heart, even as he trained in the spirit realm. There was a connection between them that went beyond words, beyond logic. It was as if their spirits were intertwined in some unseen way, each protecting the other in the face of growing darkness.

As the phantoms continued their assault, Tuwa began to grow more adept at wielding her radiant powers. She felt herself becoming stronger, more confident in her ability to protect him. Her light blazed brighter with each passing moment, pushing back the encroaching darkness. But it wasn't just her power that kept her going—it was Hansin. Every time she looked at him, every time she felt his presence, she remembered why she was here. She was the Radiant Overseer. She was here to protect him, to help him fulfill his destiny.

The battle continued for hours, and the phantoms kept returning, but Tuwa did not falter. Her energy was unwavering, her determination impenetrable. Finally, with one last blast of radiant light, the phantoms shrieked in terror and vanished into the void, defeated for now.

Exhausted, Tuwa sank to her knees beside Hansin's still form, her breathing heavy but steady. She wiped the sweat from her brow, her hands shaking slightly from the strain of the battle. She glanced at Hansin, her heart swelling with something she couldn't quite explain. The connection between them had grown stronger, more palpable, and with it, something more—a feeling, a sense of warmth that filled the space between them.

Tuwa had always kept her emotions in check, never allowing herself to be vulnerable, never letting anyone get too close. But there was something about Hansin, something about the way he trusted her, believed in her, that made her feel differently. It wasn't just about protecting him anymore. It was about standing by him, supporting him, being part of something bigger than herself.

She looked down at him, her gaze softening, and for the first time, she allowed herself to feel what she had been denying for so long. It wasn't just admiration she felt—it was a deep, growing affection. Something more than what she had been willing to admit. She didn't understand it fully, but she couldn't deny the pull she felt toward him. As she sat there, her heart racing, she realized that this wasn't just about duty anymore. There was something deeper between them, something that could change everything.

Tuwa gently placed a hand on Hansin's shoulder, her touch tender but firm. She would protect him, yes. But now, more than ever, she felt the responsibility to be there for him in every way. Whatever their journey held, she would walk beside him, not just as his protector, but as someone who, in time, might come to believe in the Divine as he did.

And in that moment, she realized she wasn't just protecting him—she was beginning to fall for him.

As Hansin's body remained still, his mind journeying through realms beyond their reach, Tuwa stood as his guardian, ready to face whatever came next. The Phantom Legionnaires had retreated for now, but there was more danger on the horizon. Yet, as she gazed down at Hansin, her heart steady, she knew one thing for certain: she would never leave him, no matter the cost.

***

One evening, as Hansin sat in his room, trying to study but feeling the strain of his double life, Tuwa spoke to him from her place near his bed, watching him with an intensity that both comforted and unnerved him.

"Hansin, you cannot do this alone," Tuwa said, her voice calm but firm. *"The Divine has chosen you, but it is not just you who will protect the balance between the realms. You must trust in those around you. You must trust in me."*

Hansin sighed, rubbing his forehead in frustration. *"I'm trying. But it's harder than I imagined. School is becoming a distant memory, and my family... I don't want to let them down. I can feel the distance growing between us."*

"Your family is a part of this journey too," Tuwa reassured him. *"They have always known, even if they didn't understand, that you were destined for something greater. You are not alone, Hansin. You never were."*

But despite Tuwa's calming words, Hansin couldn't shake the growing sense of urgency. Jezebell's Phantom Legionnaires were closing in, and he could feel their presence lurking just beyond the edge of his awareness. Their cold, malevolent energy seeped through the thin veil between the realms, like shadows stretching across the horizon. The air around him grew heavier as he meditated, his mind trying to focus amidst the chaos that surrounded him. Even as he tried to deepen his connection to the Divine, the darkness encroached on his every thought, a constant reminder of the growing threat he faced.

Tuwa stood guard over his physical body in the spirit realm, her presence a steady beacon of light that kept the phantoms at bay. She was the only thing standing between Hansin and the relentless forces of Jezebell. But even her radiant strength couldn't shield him forever. Hansin knew that with each passing hour spent in the spirit realm, his body in the physical realm became more vulnerable to the attack.

"Focus, Hansin," Tuwa's voice echoed in his mind, soothing yet firm. *"You are not alone. The Divine is with you, and so am I. Trust in that."*

Her words brought him some comfort, but they didn't alleviate the gnawing feeling that something was wrong. He could feel the Phantom Legionnaires moving in, their eerie whispers creeping into his awareness. He had learned enough about their tactics—how they attacked from the shadows, feeding on doubt and fear, manipulating those who weren't prepared. He had trained for this moment, but it felt as if the walls were closing in.

In the realm of the expired, Hansin sought to refine his powers, his connection with the Divine growing stronger each day. The realm was a place where spirits of the past lingered, where the boundaries between time and space seemed to collapse. Here, he learned to manipulate the astral energies that flowed through him and the elements, channeling them into defensive barriers that could shield his mind from the phantoms' influence. Yet, even as he practiced these techniques, he knew that the real battle lay ahead.

His training was not just to protect himself—it was to protect those he loved, to ensure that he could fight back when the time came.

Amidst these struggles, Hansin's bond with Yuppi, the spirit fox, deepened. Yuppi, once an unexpected ally, had become a trusted friend. With his ability to sense the ebb and flow of spiritual energy, Yuppi proved invaluable in the spirit realm, helping Hansin detect the subtle movements of the Phantom Legionnaires and guiding him through some of the more dangerous corners of the realm. The fox's small, glowing form darted through the spectral landscapes with ease, and Hansin found comfort in his presence, his warmth a reminder of the world he was fighting for.

One day, as Hansin and Yuppi trained together in the misty plains of the spirit realm, he felt an unexpected surge of energy. He stood, feet planted firmly on the ground, drawing in the astral energy that hummed beneath his feet.

"Do you feel that?" Hansin asked, his voice barely above a whisper.

Yuppi tilted his head, his luminous eyes reflecting the strange lights that pulsed through the mist. *"Yes, the balance shifts. Your connection is growing stronger. You are almost ready, Hansin."*

His heart quickened. He had been training for this moment—for the moment when he could stand against the forces of darkness, when he could become the guardian his people needed. His mind shifted focus, his will bending towards the task ahead.

In the spirit realm, his enemies could not harm him directly, but their influence was everywhere. He could feel their whispers tugging at his mind, tempting him to stray from his path. But with each day, his connection with the Divine became more unbreakable. He could sense Tuwa's presence, distant yet constant, always watching over him.

The more he trained, the more Hansin realized how deeply his fate was intertwined with Tuwa's. As his bond with her strengthened, so did his resolve. He could feel her power growing alongside his own. Together, they would protect the realms, together, they would face Jezebell.

And as the Phantom Legionnaires continued to move closer, Hansin knew that it was no longer a question of *if* they would attack, but when. Yet, despite the mounting danger, his faith in the Divine and the growing strength of his allies gave him hope. He wasn't alone. And as the time for his final trial drew near, he would be ready.

***

Meanwhile, Keanu's jealousy festered, twisting his heart in ways Hansin could never have anticipated. From the moment Tuwa, the Radiant Overseer, had appeared, Keanu felt a pull toward her—something he couldn't deny. At first sight, his heart had desired her, an infatuation that burned brighter with each passing day. But when Tuwa made it clear that her heart belonged to Hansin, that affection shifting toward his younger brother instead of him, a deep bitterness took root in Keanu's chest.

The bond between Hansin and Tuwa—both protector and protectorate—was something Keanu could not ignore. He had always been the older brother, the one who had been looked to for guidance, the one who was supposed to be the stronger of the two. Yet, Hansin's role as the Astral Guardian had somehow eclipsed him. Not only did Hansin now share an unbreakable divine connection with Tuwa, but it was that very connection that deepened Keanu's resentment.

Keanu had always wanted to be the one who held power, the one who would lead, but now, it seemed, Hansin had everything—strength, purpose, and Tuwa's devotion. The jealousy he felt toward his brother grew with each day, and soon it became clear to him that he could no longer stand idly by while Hansin continued to rise.

Late one night, as Keanu wandered through the dimly lit halls of their home, the ever-present shadow of Jezebell's influence crept into his mind. The Phantom Legionnaires had already begun whispering into his thoughts, preying on his vulnerabilities and insecurities. They spoke of power, of revenge, and of a world where Hansin's destiny was no longer secure. They spoke of a chance for Keanu to claim his own place in this battle, and claim Tuwa's heart as well—if only he would betray his brother and join them.

The darkness in Keanu's heart hardened as the words of Jezebell's legion became clearer. The promise of strength, the offer of a life where he was no longer overshadowed by Hansin's destiny, tugged at his soul. His desire for power clouded his better judgment, and with every whisper, the seed of betrayal took root.

With a quiet, bitter laugh, Keanu made his decision. He would no longer stand in the shadow of his brother's destiny. He would align himself with the forces that promised him the power he craved, even if it meant betraying the very family that had raised him, even if it meant becoming a tool in Jezebell's dark army.

"I'll do whatever it takes," Keanu whispered to the shadows, a sneer curling on his lips as he let go of any lingering doubts. The decision had been made—his jealousy would drive him forward, and no bond, not even the love he had once shared with his brother, would stop him.

In that moment, Keanu cast aside any trace of hesitation. The Phantom Legionnaires had found a willing recruit in him, and now, his path was set. His jealousy, fueled by unrequited desire and the bitterness of feeling overlooked, had led him into the arms of darkness. And with his betrayal, Hansin's struggle would become all the more dire.

***

As Hansin's academic performance continued to deteriorate, the staff at school began to take notice. His teachers whispered behind closed doors about the sudden drop in his grades, and counselors started requesting meetings with his family. Hansin knew he was walking a thin line between his destiny and his obligations in the physical world, but the pressure was starting to crack him. Tuwa, though ever vigilant, could only do so much to shield him from the consequences of his neglect.

And then came the moment when everything shifted.

Jezebell's Phantom Legionnaires had finally turned their focus to Hansin directly, moving swiftly and with deadly precision. The forces of darkness had infiltrated the physical realm, creeping silently through the cracks between worlds, their eyes fixed firmly on him. They knew that Hansin, though now a powerful Astral Guardian, remained vulnerable in the physical realm. His body, while it held great potential, was a mere vessel for his true power—a power he could only tap into while training and meditating within the spirit realms. The Phantom Legionnaires saw this weakness, and with it, they saw an opportunity to strike.

Their attack was not limited to Hansin alone. Jezebell's dark forces had learned long ago that breaking a person required breaking those they held dear. Friends, classmates, even teachers—anyone who was within range, who had even the slightest connection to Hansin, was now a potential target. The Phantom Legionnaires sought to weaken Hansin by turning his closest allies against him or breaking them through fear, manipulation, and violence.

Each day, Hansin felt the weight of this battle press down on him more heavily. His Radiant Overseer, Tuwa, was resolute in her duty to protect him. She fought alongside him in the spirit realm, shielding his vulnerable body with her radiant power, but even her strength had its limits. As the Phantom Legionnaires encroached further into the physical realm, their dark influence grew more pervasive, and her defenses began to show cracks.

Tuwa's power was vast—she was a force of light, unmatched in the physical realm—but she was not invincible. The toll of constantly protecting Hansin while he was in a vulnerable state began to show. She had been tasked with keeping Hansin safe while he meditated and trained in the spirit realms, but it wasn't enough. The Phantom Legionnaires were relentless. Each new attack they launched was more coordinated, more insidious. They began targeting those closest to him, manipulating their minds and emotions, turning his friends and loved ones against him without them even realizing it.

Hansin, despite his growing power, found himself overwhelmed. He couldn't fight back in the way he knew he needed to. His heart and mind were split between the physical and spirit realms, constantly shifting as he tried to protect his body while training to battle Jezebell's forces. Every time he entered the spirit realm to fight off the phantoms, he was momentarily disconnected from the physical realm—leaving his body open to attack, leaving those around him vulnerable. His energy drained with every shift, his strength worn thin by the constant demands of both realms.

Mentally, the toll was even worse. His mind raced with constant vigilance, fighting against the darkness and the exhaustion that threatened to overtake him. He had to constantly hide his true nature, downplay his growing powers, while still protecting those around him. If anyone in his school, in his life, found out what he was really capable of, it would not only put them in danger but could ruin everything he was working for. But that wasn't his only burden. Every time he entered the spirit realm to battle the phantoms, he could feel the physical toll it took on his body—he was pushed to his limits, but he could not afford to stop.

He could feel his physical body weakening, his body growing weary as his soul fought in both realms. His schoolwork began to suffer, his relationships strained. Friends who once looked up to him began pulling away, unable to understand why he was acting strange, why he was distant. His teachers noticed the change in his focus and performance, and they began to ask questions he couldn't answer. But Hansin could only retreat deeper into himself, trying to manage the strain in silence. His true struggle—his battle to protect his loved ones, his fight against Jezebell's forces—was something he couldn't share, couldn't explain.

And still, the attacks came. Each day brought new challenges, and Hansin could feel the pressure of the world around him tightening like a vice. Every time he meditated, every time he crossed between realms, he feared what he might come back to in the physical world. He could no longer pretend that everything would be okay.

The Phantom Legionnaires were no longer a distant threat—they were here, now, and they were closing in, circling like vultures around a wounded prey.

Tuwa remained by his side, her presence a beacon of light in the overwhelming darkness, but even she was struggling to keep up with the constant onslaught. The weight of their bond—of his need for her protection—began to take its toll on her as well. She was only one person, and her focus was divided. Her ability to shield him was growing weaker, stretched thin by the growing attacks.

For Hansin, the battle was no longer just about training—it was about survival. He couldn't hide his true purpose forever, but he didn't know how much longer he could go on at this pace. Each battle with Jezebell's forces was another reminder of how much was at stake, how much he had yet to learn. The longer he stayed in the physical realm, the more dangerous it became—not just for him, but for those he cared about.

The tension was unbearable, and it seemed the more he fought, the more drained he became, both physically and mentally. Yet, despite the odds, Hansin kept pressing forward, knowing that his true calling was only beginning, and that no matter how difficult the path ahead seemed, he could not afford to stop.

***

Meanwhile, Keanu, his mind twisted with jealousy and the influence of Jezebell's forces, began to set his plan in motion. He would watch Hansin fall, his family's legacy lost to the corruption of Jezebell's power, and he would be the one to rise from the ashes. The betrayal was nearly complete, and Keanu no longer cared who or what he had to destroy to claim the power that had always eluded him.

The struggle was no longer just about Hansin's training and divine calling. It was about family, loyalty, and the ultimate cost of betrayal. And as Hansin's enemies closed in, he would soon discover that even those closest to him could become the most dangerous threats.

"Hansin," Tuwa's voice broke through his thoughts as the storm of enemies gathered around them. *"We must stay united. We must trust in the Divine's plan."*

Hansin nodded, his resolve hardening as he prepared for the trials ahead. The forces of darkness were closing in, and the line between ally and enemy was becoming dangerously blurred.

Chapter 5: Reflections of Betrayal

The weight of the past year had settled heavily on Hansin's shoulders. He was no longer the inexperienced Astral Guardian who had first stepped into his role—he was now at his full strength, a formidable force in both the physical and spirit realms. Protector of both realms. His bond with Tuwa had deepened, and the two had become not just partners in battle, but a couple bound by the fires of shared purpose, faith, and love. Together, they were unstoppable—each day, each battle, proving their strength and devotion to one another and to the Divine. But despite their power and unity, a shadow lingered in Hansin's heart, a heaviness he couldn't shake.

It had been a year since Hansin had fully come into his powers, and yet the losses he had suffered continued to haunt him. The death of his beloved great-grandmother, a woman who had been a guiding force in his life, had struck him to his core. She had been taken from him by a phantom-possessed individual, someone who had once been innocent—until the dark influence of Jezebell's Phantom Legionnaires had corrupted them. Worse yet, Hansin knew now that it was his own brother, Keanu, who had been complicit in her death, working directly with Jezebell to orchestrate the tragedy with hopes of breaking Hansin.

The truth had shattered Hansin. The betrayal cut deeper than any wound he had faced in battle. Keanu, his older brother, had always been a part of his life—a figure Hansin had looked up to, someone he had trusted with his heart. But now, Keanu was working directly under Jezebell's command, wielding dark forces abilities to corrupt the world around him, to fight against Hansin and everything he stood for.

Hansin couldn't believe it. He refused to, at first. But the evidence was undeniable. Keanu's allegiance to Jezebell, his embrace of darkness and destruction, had become all too clear. The whispers of betrayal were now facts, and the weight of that truth threatened to crush him. He could no longer look at his brother the same way. Their bond, once inseparable, had now been broken beyond repair.

Despite the overwhelming grief and anger, Hansin held fast to his faith in the Divine. The loss of his great-grandmother, the crushing blow of Keanu's betrayal—it all tested his resolve, but Hansin knew that his calling came with great responsibility. He understood that the path of an Astral Guardian was fraught with loss, sacrifice, and hardship. It was a burden he had to bear, not just for himself, but for the world.

The only constants left in his life were his mother, Tuwa, and the Divine. These were the only three he could trust without hesitation. His mother had been his rock, even as she grieved alongside him. Tuwa, his partner in both love and battle, was always by his side, offering unwavering support and strength. Together, they had become a formidable force, but Hansin knew that the coming conflict—one that would pit him directly against his brother—was inevitable.

***

The air around them crackled with tension as Hansin and Keanu stood face to face. The battlefield was set, a barren wasteland where the forces of light and dark would collide. Hansin could feel the weight of the moment, the silence between them louder than any words they could exchange. The memory of his brother—the boy who had once stood by his side—felt like a distant dream. In its place stood a dark force, corrupted by Jezebell's power, an enemy that Hansin could no longer recognize.

Keanu's eyes, once warm and familiar, now burned with an icy, malevolent fire. His connection to Jezebell had granted him dark elemental powers that twisted the fabric of the world itself. Darkness radiated from him, bending the air around them, and the ground beneath his feet seemed to writhe and tremble in response to his corrupted energy. Keanu's hands crackled with shadows as if they were alive, swirling with twisted blackness that threatened to devour everything in its path.

"Hansin..." Keanu's voice was a low growl, a mockery of the brotherly affection they once shared. *"You still think you can save me? Your weak faith won't change anything. The darkness has already claimed me. It's time for you to face that truth."*

Hansin's chest tightened. He wanted to deny it. He wanted to reach through the veil of darkness and pull his brother back, to remind him of their shared past, the bond they had once shared, the faith in the Divine Keanu once held. But he knew, deep down, that Keanu had made his choice. The weight of that truth crushed Hansin, but he stood firm. He was not just an Astral Guardian—he was the protector of this world, and he could no longer let his brother's betrayal cloud his duty.

With a swift movement, Hansin summoned his powers, the radiant energy of light and fire converging in his palms. His aura flared brightly, pushing against the suffocating darkness Keanu exuded. Fire, the element of transformation and purification, roared to life in his hands, pushing back the shadows that swarmed around him. He felt the power surge within him—the full strength of his training, of his legacy.

Keanu sneered, dark energy swirling around him. In an instant, he unleashed a barrage of shadow strikes, the tendrils of darkness shooting forward like arrows aimed at Hansin. The air around them turned cold, the light of the world dimming as Keanu's power seeped into the fabric of reality itself.

Hansin deflected the shadows with his flame-infused shield, the heat of his fire scorching the tendrils as they collided. The ground trembled beneath their feet, and flashes of light and dark filled the air as the two forces collided in an explosive clash. Hansin's elemental mastery was undeniable—his control over fire, light, and the spirit realm had become near absolute. But Keanu... Keanu was different now. His abilities had been twisted by Jezebell's influence, and the power he wielded was unnatural, draining the very energy of the world around him.

Hansin pressed forward, but the emotional weight of the battle was unbearable. Every blow he struck, every shadow he fought, felt like a strike against the brother he had once known, the family he had once cherished. The pain of the betrayal clouded his mind, his heart heavy with regret. He wasn't sure how much longer he could continue to fight.

"I can't do this," Hansin muttered to himself, the conflict within him growing

too powerful to ignore. *"I can't destroy him..."*

Tuwa, standing just behind him, felt his hesitation. Their connection, honed through years of shared experiences and now enhanced by their telekinetic communication, was palpable. It was as if their minds were intertwined, their thoughts flowing seamlessly from one to the other. Her presence was a balm to his soul, a steady anchor in the storm of his emotions. Through their mental link, she could feel his internal struggle, the conflict raging inside him. She understood his pain. She understood the weight of the betrayal Hansin carried, the love he still felt for Keanu, even now.

"Hansin," Tuwa's voice echoed in his mind, soft yet unwavering, filled with love and clarity. *"This is not your fight to finish. You've done everything you could*

for Keanu. But now... now it's time for me to protect you, to protect everything we've built. To protect you the way you've protected me."

Hansin's heart twisted at the sound of her words. He could feel her love, her strength, and the resolve that filled her being. He felt her steady presence like a beacon in the chaos of his emotions. In her eyes, when he glanced at her, he saw not only a warrior's strength but the power of love, of faith, and a willingness to do what was necessary, no matter the cost. She was ready. She was his assigned protector, as much as he had tried to protect her in the past.

He hesitated for just a moment longer, his gaze lingering on Keanu—on the brother he had once known. But deep down, Hansin understood the truth. The brother he had loved was gone, consumed by darkness. It was time to let go. With a final, lingering thought of regret, Hansin stepped back.

He didn't need to speak the words aloud. Tuwa understood. He had done everything he could, and now, it was time for her to take over.

The battle between Tuwa and Keanu erupted like a storm. The forces of light and dark clashed with an intensity that shook the very foundations of the world. Tuwa's powers of light flared to life, her form glowing with radiant energy. Her hands extended, and the pure, white light that poured from them seemed to pierce the very darkness that Keanu commanded. She moved with the grace of a warrior of the Divine, striking with precision and power.

With a swift motion, Tuwa unleashed a wave of blinding light, a beam that cut through the shadows and struck Keanu directly. The impact caused the ground beneath them to shudder, but Keanu was quick to retaliate. He summoned a dark vortex, a swirling maelstrom of shadows that engulfed the light and pulled it into a spiraling abyss. The vortex distorted the very fabric of reality, causing the sky to darken as the winds howled in response.

Tuwa didn't falter. She summoned the full strength of her light—she was a beacon of hope, and she would not let Keanu's darkness snuff it out. She channeled her power into a massive dome of light, surrounding them both with an impenetrable force. The light pulsed, its brilliance overwhelming the dark vortex, pushing Keanu's dark forces back with relentless force.

But Keanu fought back with everything he had. His shadow tendrils lashed out, tearing at the edges of the light barrier, trying to rip it apart. The air crackled as the two forces collided, a battle of wills and elemental powers.

Tuwa's resolve was unshakable. She focused all of her energy into the center of the light, creating a brilliant sphere of radiant energy. The sphere expanded, blinding in its intensity, forcing Keanu to retreat as it burned through the darkness he had become. His body began to twitch and convulse as the overpowering divine light stripped him of his dark abilities, peeling back the layers of corruption that Jezebell had placed upon him.

Keanu fell to his knees, gasping, his eyes wild with shock and fury. His once-powerful dark energy had been completely neutralized, the light of Tuwa's power breaking the hold that Jezebell had on him. Keanu's powers were stripped away—the force of the light had purged the darkness that had consumed him.

Hansin stepped forward slowly, his heart torn. His brother, once a powerful ally, was now a shadow of the man he had known. But Hansin's love for him was not enough to reverse the consequences of Keanu's choices.

As the dust settled, Keanu, now powerless, glared at them both, his body trembling from the loss of his dark powers. His eyes met Hansin's one last time—an unspoken understanding between them. Keanu's path had led him here, but Hansin had not given up on the possibility of his redemption.

Hansin and Tuwa stood together, their bond stronger than ever, but the silence between them was heavy with the weight of all that had been lost. The battle was over, but the cost of victory lingered, leaving behind only the quiet reflection of the brother Hansin had lost.

Tuwa approached Keanu, and with one swift movement rendered him unconscious.

The silence that followed was deafening. Hansin's heart ached, but there was no joy in their victory—only the quiet reflection of the brother Hansin had lost, the family that had been shattered by the forces of darkness.

As Tuwa stood over the fallen Keanu, Hansin stepped forward, their minds once again intertwined through their telekinetic link. He could feel her emotions, the reluctance and sorrow in her heart as she gazed upon the brother he had once loved.

"We did what we had to, Hansin," she said softly in his mind, her voice a quiet

echo in the silence. *"But it doesn't make it any easier."*

The battle had ended, but the silence that followed was not one of peace. The world had shifted, and Hansin's heart felt as if it were trapped between two realms—his brother's betrayal and the weight of the world's suffering pressing down on him. Keanu, no longer the brother he had once known, was now imprisoned in the Sacred Grounds, sealed away by Tuwa's radiant light. The darkness that had consumed him was locked away, beyond the reach of Jezebell's influence, but the victory was hollow.

Keanu was not dead. His life was preserved, but so was his corruption—a corruption Hansin could not undo. The pain of watching his brother's descent into darkness was still fresh, but Tuwa's strength had brought him some semblance of peace. She had protected him, both physically and emotionally, through it all, and now, she stood by his side, a steady beacon in the storm.

But even her light couldn't chase away the shadows that lingered in Hansin's heart. The world around them was falling apart. Jezebell's influence had reached far beyond their immediate circle, tearing at the fabric of society. Crime was at an all-time high. Innocent lives were lost daily, their blood spilling onto the streets, and it was all part of Jezebell's plan to wear Hansin down. She had hoped to break Hansin, to overwhelm him with responsibility until his spirit cracked under the pressure.

And yet, Hansin's resolve remained unbroken, even though it was tested at every turn. He had lost so much—his grandmother, his trust in his brother, and the hope that the family they had once been could be restored. But his faith in the Divine remained. He knew the cost of his calling, and though the weight of it was almost too much to bear, he would not abandon it. He couldn't.

It was in these moments of quiet reflection, standing beside Tuwa as they gazed out over the land, that Hansin made his decision. The battle against Jezebell was no longer just about protecting those he loved—it was about ending her reign of terror. He could no longer stand by as she consumed the world around him. He could no longer carry the burden of watching innocents suffer in the name of her corruption.

The time had come to face her.

"Hansin," Tuwa's voice broke through his thoughts, and he turned to meet her gaze. *"I know what you're thinking. And I stand with you. Whatever comes next, we face it together."*

Her words grounded him. Her light, her unwavering faith, was the anchor he needed to move forward. The fight with Keanu, the loss of family, the betrayal—it was all leading to this moment. And as Jezebell's forces continued to spiral out of control, Hansin knew there was no turning back.

"She's waiting for us, isn't she?" Hansin said, his voice low and steady.

Tuwa nodded, her eyes flashing with determination. *"She's been waiting for the moment when you'd finally come to terms with what's been lost. But she won't break us. Not now. Not ever."*

Hansin's heart clenched with the weight of it all, but he knew she was right. Jezebell wanted his power—she wanted his strength to escape the spirit realm and plunge the world into eternal darkness. He had faced betrayal, loss, and unimaginable pain, but now, he would face the source of it all.

The final battle was coming.

Chapter 6: Legacy of Resilience

The final showdown with Jezebell had come at last, and Hansin felt every ounce of weight in his bones as he faced her, knowing that this battle would determine the fate of both realms. The air was thick with tension, crackling with the essence of the ancient war between light and dark. Jezebell stood before him, her form a swirling mass of shadows and malevolent energy, a dark smile playing on her lips. She had been waiting for this moment—waiting to drain him of his power, to feast on his strength and finally escape the confines of the spirit realm.

"You're too late, young guardian," Jezebell sneered, her voice like a cold wind. *"The spirit realm bow to me, and soon the physical realm to follow, you will be nothing more than a failed memory."*

Her laughter echoed in the air, but Hansin did not flinch. He knew the stakes, and he was ready to fight—he would not let her consume the realm, nor would he allow her to twist everything he loved into shadows. His body glowed with the radiant energy of his Astral powers, a shimmering light of pure resolve that reflected his commitment to the light. But this time, he was more than just an Astral Guardian. He was the embodiment of the elements, every fiber of his being an extension of the natural world.

Jezebell's forces were overwhelming. Her phantom legions, vast and relentless, materialized from the shadows, their forms shifting like wisps of smoke, each one an echo of her dark magic. They surrounded Hansin, their eyes burning with an unnatural light. He had fought countless battles, but this one—this was different. The weight of it pressed on him from every angle.

Hansin's pulse raced as he gathered his elemental abilities, summoning the power of the Earth beneath his feet. The ground trembled, and the very stones around him cracked and erupted, forming towering walls of rock and earth that shielded him from the phantom attacks. He raised his arms, the rocks shifting and flowing like an extension of his will, hurling jagged spikes toward the advancing legion.

The earth rumbled, sending shockwaves through the realm, and the phantom legions faltered, their ethereal forms rippling with discomfort. But Jezebell, unfazed, pushed forward, her dark energy surging in waves that shattered the earth around Hansin.

"Is that all you have, boy?" she taunted, her voice dripping with contempt. *"You will fall like all the others."*

Hansin's heart raced. He could feel the weight of her words, but he couldn't let her win. Summoning the air, he whipped his hands forward, sending gusts of wind that twisted fire and howled with fury. He controlled it, shaping the winds to create a protective vortex around him, deflecting the phantoms' attacks as they lunged.

The winds howled like a furious storm, sending the phantom legions scattering, but they quickly regrouped, undeterred. Jezebell's laugh grew louder, her power feeding off the phantoms' despair and pain.

"You cannot defeat me with these tricks, Hansin," Jezebell hissed, her form shifting like smoke, her eyes glowing with the intensity of her dark power. *"I*

have harnessed the power of the corrupted for centuries. You are nothing."

Hansin's pulse thundered in his ears. He knew she was right—he couldn't fight her alone with his elemental powers. Her darkness was too powerful, her ability to drain his strength too overwhelming. He could feel her claws sinking deeper into his energy, her corruption feeding off his light. But just as Hansin's hope began to wane, a familiar presence surged in the spirit realm.

Yuppi, the spirit fox, materialized at his side. With a brilliant flash of radiant light, Yuppi unleashed a blast of fire, searing through the phantom legions with a force that sent them scattering. The fox's form was agile and powerful, his flames dancing in the air as he joined Hansin in the fight.

"We fight together, Hansin!" Yuppi's voice echoed in his mind, his fiery tail blazing behind him.

With Yuppi's assistance and some joining allies of the spirit realm, the phantoms faltered. Their movements slowed, their attacks disorganized as Hansin and Yuppi fought side by side. But Jezebell's wrath only grew stronger, and Hansin knew that even with Yuppi and his allies' help, it would not be enough to defeat her. The darkness was simply too great.

"You cannot win, child," Jezebell spat, her hands crackling with darkness as she began to absorb the power from the phantoms, growing in strength with every moment. Her form became more terrifying—twisted, immense, and unstoppable. Her power lashed out, overwhelming Hansin's defenses,

sending shockwaves of dark energy through the air.

Hansin's body buckled under the force of her assault. His strength began to falter. He could feel his powers slipping away, his connection to the elements weakening with every moment. The light that had once burned so brightly within him now flickered, dimming beneath the crushing weight of Jezebell's power, he could feel his life slowly being drained, slipping away moment by moment.

***

Back in the physical realm, Tuwa felt the shift in their connection, the bond between them flickering as Hansin faltered. She could sense his pain, the struggle he was enduring. The connection they had forged, their telekinetic bond, was more than just a means of communication—it was the tether that linked their souls, and in this

141

moment, she could feel his life slipping away.

She knew what she had to do.

Tuwa's resolve hardened, her decision made with a clarity that only came from pure faith and fervent love. She stepped forward, her heart pounding in her chest as she closed her eyes and called upon the Divine. Her powers, radiant and pure, surged within her as she poured them into Hansin, knowing that this sacrifice was her only hope to save him. She would give everything—her strength, her light, her very essence—to save him.

"Hansin, hold on," she thought to him, her telekinetic voice echoing in his mind. *"You are not alone. I'm with you. Always."*

In the spirit realm, Hansin felt the warmth of her light flood through him.

Her sacrifice was felt deep within his soul, a wave of power that surged through his body, reigniting the flame of his Astral abilities. The darkness that had been closing in on him faltered for a moment as the power from Tuwa coursed through him. The boost of energy, pure and untainted, gave him the strength to rise once more.

But even with this newfound power, Jezebell was not finished. The intensity of their battle had left its mark on both of them, but especially Hansin. His body trembled under the strain of the elements he had wielded so recklessly, and the weight of his sacrifices pressed down on him like an unyielding mountain. Jezebell, her face twisted with fury, refused to yield. Her dark power pulsed around her like an insatiable beast, and with an enraged scream that shattered the very air between them, she began to gather her strength for one final, devastating blow.

Hansin staggered, barely able to keep his footing as the world seemed to tilt around him. He could feel the edges of his consciousness slipping, his body fighting against the immense toll this battle had taken. But his heart burned with an unshakable resolve. He would not fall here. Not when everything was at stake. Not when the realms were hanging in the balance.

Jezebell's shadowed form stretched and twisted, distorting as it grew in power. Her tendrils of darkness lashed out, crackling with an energy that threatened to consume him entirely. The very air around her became charged with malignant intent, and Hansin could feel the ground beneath him rumble as if even the realm itself feared her final attack. Her eyes blazed with a cold, merciless fire as she drew all of her corrupted power into a swirling vortex of shadows.

"You think you can defeat me, boy?" Jezebell hissed, her voice a guttural snarl. *"I am darkness incarnate, the void from which corrupted life springs and to which it returns. You are nothing."*

Hansin's pulse thundered in his ears. He had nothing left, not physically, not even spiritually. His powers were at their breaking point. But then, he remembered Tuwa—her sacrifice, her love, her light. The power that surged through him now was not just his own; it was Tuwa's, an unyielding force of divine grace. He could feel her presence beside him, like an unbreakable tether that refused to let him fall.

He stood tall, refusing to give in, his hand raised, the light within him flickering but refusing to die. As the darkness swirled around him, his heart pounded with the weight of the moment, and his mind cried out to the Divine. *"Lord, hear me. I am but Your vessel, Your servant. Through every trial, You have guided me. Now, in the face of this abyss, I call upon Your strength, Your light. Help me, Divine Father, for I am nothing without You. I stand as a reflection of Your will. Grant me the power to defeat this darkness, as Jesus defeated Satan, to protect those I love, and to restore what has been broken. Let Your light shine through me and consume the shadows. I place my faith in You."*

He called on every ounce of his power, every breath, every heartbeat, and focused on the elements, trusting in the Divine to deliver him. The earth beneath his feet shuddered with the weight of his command, and the air around him crackled as the fire and water he conjured mingled in a dance of light and shadow. His energy stretched outward, a beacon of brilliant power that threatened to blind the very darkness itself.

With a guttural cry, Hansin released the full force of his power. He summoned the elements in their entirety—the earth cracked beneath him, sending jagged pillars of stone into the air. His telekinetic powers wove through the space around him, manipulating the very fabric of the realm to shape his energy into a brilliant sphere of light. The flames he conjured roared with fury, their heat intense enough to burn the very fabric of the spirit realm. Water surged from the depths of the ether, crashing against the shadows in a torrent of force. Air whipped through the battlefield, creating a violent vortex that howled in harmony with the storm of light Hansin had unleashed.

The world trembled as Hansin's body glowed with divine power, his form now a living embodiment of the elements enhanced with the favor of the Divine. Light poured from him in streams so pure, so radiant, that it tore through the oppressive darkness like a bolt of lightning. Jezebell screamed as the light engulfed her, her form beginning to distort and crack under the pressure. Her power, immense and unyielding, recoiled in the face of the overwhelming divine energy that Hansin had become.

"You cannot win," Jezebell spat, her voice a shrill rasp, twisting in the air. *"I am the darkness! You will never defeat me!"*

"I will win, just as Jesus defeated Satan when He poured out His blood upon the cross!," Hansin declared, his voice firm, unwavering. *"I will defeat you just the*

*same, not by might or my power, but by
the Divine!"*

Hansin's eyes, now ablaze with the
intensity of doing the Divine's will,
burned with a quiet, unshakable faith.
He could feel his powers being drained
by the intense struggle, yet something
deeper than his physical strength
surged within him. The weight of his
body threatened to collapse under the
pressure, but his spirit remained
steadfast. He had been brought to this
moment for a reason. The Divine was
with him, and that truth was undeniable.

His every nerve screamed in agony as
Jezebell's shadow continued to press
against him, but Hansin refused to
relent. His spirit burned brighter, pushing
against the overwhelming darkness that
sought to consume him. This was the
moment of truth—the final stand.

With one last push, Hansin focused all of his strength, directing every last ounce of his power toward Jezebell. His mind called upon the elements—the earth beneath him rose in response, cracking and shifting, while the air crackled with electric charge. The flames that licked at his fingertips ignited the very air around him, while the waters surged in a wild dance of light and shadow. His body, though breaking, was in perfect unison with the forces he controlled. His prayer echoed through him, his heart aligned with the Divine, and he knew that this battle would end, not through his might, but through the power of his faith.

It was now or never.

The light from his body surged forward, piercing the very heart of Jezebell's shadow. She screamed in agony as the dark power that had sustained her for so long began to crumble beneath the assault. Her form, once towering and menacing, began to fracture, the very essence of her being unraveling under the relentless tide of divine light. The shadow that had once defined her was no match for the purity of Hansin's heart and the strength of his resolve.

In one final, climactic blow, Hansin poured everything he had left into the attack. The light erupted from him in a dazzling explosion, so brilliant it tore through the very fabric of the spirit realm itself. The ground quaked, the air burned, and the shadows disintegrated in an instant. Jezebell's form crumbled to dust, her malevolent power dissipating into the ether, leaving behind only the faintest echo of her existence.

The silence that followed was deafening. The battle was over. The darkness had been vanquished, and

Hansin stood victorious—but at a great cost. His body shook with exhaustion, his powers spent, but his heart swelled with the knowledge that the realms were safe once again.

As the dust settled and the realms began to heal, Hansin collapsed to his knees, breathing heavily. His body, broken and battered, could not withstand the toll of the battle much longer. But the light that had guided him—Tuwa's sacrifice, the divine power within him—burned brighter than ever. And in that light, Hansin knew that no matter how great the darkness, no matter how overwhelming the struggle, there was always hope, always a way to overcome.

Jezebell had been defeated. The balance had been restored.

But Hansin's journey was far from over. The realms would need rebuilding, and his allies would need his strength. The echoes of Keanu's betrayal still lingered in his heart, and the weight of his uncertain future pressed heavily on his shoulders. Yet, as he looked to the horizon, he felt the embers of hope stir within him, knowing that whatever lay ahead, he would face it with unwavering faith.

The battle for the spirit realm was over. But the true test of his legacy, and the legacy of resilience he carried within, was just beginning.

Hansin stood over her fallen form, panting, bloodied, and bruised. The spirit realm around them began to shift, the air clearing as Jezebell's influence was finally broken. The peace that had been absent for so long was restored, but at a great cost. Hansin could feel the weight of the victory, the toll it had taken on him, but the burden of the future loomed even larger.

With Jezebell defeated and balance restored, Hansin and his allies returned to the physical realm. Together, they began the difficult task of rebuilding—of repairing the damage caused by Jezebell's forces and strengthening the defenses of both realms. The work was monumental, but Hansin felt the hope of a new beginning.

Yet, even in the quiet aftermath, Hansin could not shake the turmoil within him. Keanu's betrayal still haunted him, the weight of his brother's choices a constant reminder of the broken family he had once known. His future, too, remained uncertain. He had fought with everything he had, but the scars of the past—of loss, of betrayal—would remain with him. He had forgiven his brother, even if Keanu had not asked him to, but the scars remained.

As he looked out over the land, his heart heavy with the weight of all he had endured, he knew one thing for certain: the legacy of resilience that had been passed down to him was more than just a tale of survival. It was a legacy of faith. A legacy that, even in the face of darkness, could not be extinguished.

And no matter what lay ahead, with the help of the Divine, Hansin would continue to fight for the light.

Chapter 7: Guardian's Resolve

Hansin stood on the edge of the sacred grounds, gazing into the shimmering veil that separated the physical and Astral realms. The battle with Dyani had left scars—on the realms, on his body, and on his heart. Yet, through the pain and loss, he felt an overwhelming gratitude to the Divine. It was not by his strength, nor by his might, but by the grace and power of the Divine that victory had been secured.

He knelt in the soft, glowing grass, bowing his head in silent prayer. *Lord, I give You all the glory. This victory belongs to You alone. Thank You for Tuwa's love and sacrifice, for the strength You gave me to endure, and for the path You have set before me. Guide me as I walk it, and may my life continue to honor You.*

Years had passed since the final showdown with Dyani, and though the echoes of that battle lingered, the realms had found peace once more. The Divine, in His infinite wisdom, had not let Tuwa's sacrifice go unanswered. Shortly after Dyani's defeat, a new Radiant Overseer was chosen—Micah, a young guardian with a heart ablaze for righteousness. The blessing passed to him, and with it, the responsibility of standing by Hansin's side.

Micah quickly became more than an ally; he became a dear friend to both Hansin and Tuwa. His steadfast faith and unwavering courage were a constant source of encouragement. Together, they forged a bond of brotherhood, their combined strength a beacon of hope for the realms.

One evening, as the three sat beneath the pink skies, watching the stars dance like jewels scattered across the heavens, Micah smiled warmly. *"You know, Hansin,"* he said, his voice light yet sincere, *"I've learned so much from you and Tuwa. Your faith, your resilience—it inspires me every day."*

Hansin chuckled softly, shaking his head. *"And I've learned just as much from you, Micah. The Divine knew what He was doing when He chose you. I couldn't ask for a better Radiant Overseer or a truer friend."*

Tuwa, resting her head against Hansin's shoulder, added, *"Micah, your presence has been a blessing to us both. You've given us the chance to start a family, to build a future we never thought possible. For that, we'll always be grateful."*

Indeed, Tuwa and Hansin had begun a new chapter in their lives. With Micah standing guard as Hansin continued to serve as protector of the realms, the couple had been able to settle into a life filled with love, laughter, and hope. Yet, Hansin's duty remained. Darkness would always seek to invade, but with the Divine's light guiding him, he stood ready.

One day, as the wind carried whispers of an impending threat, Micah approached Hansin, his expression both determined and calm. *"It looks like we're needed again,"* he said, his voice steady.

Hansin nodded, a faint smile playing on his lips. *"Then we'll answer the call, as we always do. Not by might, nor by power, but by the Spirit of the Divine."*

Together, Hansin and Micah prepared to face whatever darkness loomed on the horizon. The battles would come, and the struggles would be great, but they would not stand alone. Hansin knew that his journey was far from over, yet with faith as his shield and the Divine as his guide, he was ready to face whatever lay ahead.

Thus, the legacy of the Astral Guardian endured—a testament to the power of faith, the strength of love, and the enduring light of the Divine. Hansin's story became one of hope and inspiration, a reminder to all that even in the darkest of times, the light will always prevail.

***

As we've journeyed through this story, we've witnessed the power of light overcoming darkness and transformation. The battle between good and evil is not just confined to these pages; it is a real battle we all face in our lives. In the world we live in, there are forces that seek to lead us away from what is good, pure, and holy. But there is hope, and that hope comes through a divine hero far greater than any character we could imagine.

This hero, Jesus Christ, has already won the ultimate victory over evil, He defeated Satan and death, He is freely offering us salvation, freedom, and eternal life. No matter what darkness we may face, with Jesus, we are safe. His love and grace are freely offered to all who choose to follow Him.

If you've felt the stir in your heart and are ready to accept the gift of salvation that He offers, you can pray this prayer aloud with a sincere heart:

Lord Jesus, please forgive me for anything and everything I've done that was against You and others. I repent today of all my sins, and I ask You, Jesus, to come into my heart and save me today. You said in Your word that if I confess with my mouth the Lord Jesus, and believe that He died for me and rose again, that I shall be saved. And right now, I do confess, and I make You, Jesus, my Savior and my Lord. So right now, Lord, I thank You for saving me. I thank You for forgiving me, and today, Lord, I forgive myself. Lord, I ask You to create in me a new upright heart, remove all unrighteousness from me. Now, Holy Spirit, fill me with Your presence, Your fruits, Your power, and Your glory. Use me according to the word of God. I declare as of today that every chain and stronghold is broken by the blood of the Messiah, Jesus Christ of Nazareth, my Lord. It is in Jesus' name that I pray, Amen.

If you prayed that prayer, know that you are now a child of God. Your journey has just begun, and you are not alone—Jesus is with you every step of the way through His Holy Spirit that lives within every true believer, helping you overcome the trials and temptations you may face. Just like the heroes in this story, you are protected by His love, grace, and power. Welcome to the family of believers!

Thank you so much for reading, I would greatly appreciate it if you take a moment to leave a review wherever you purchased this book and please share it with others!

Made in the USA
Columbia, SC
21 March 2025

55463875R00100